For my Bellingham family,
Roger, Bonnie, Jael & Karin DeSpain,
with love
— *P.D.*

Text © 1995 by Pleasant DeSpain.
Illustrations © 1995 by Joe Shlichta.

Published 1995 by August House LittleFolk
P.O. Box 3223, Little Rock, Arkansas 72203
501-372-5450.

Book design by Harvill Ross Studios Ltd.

Manufactured in Hong Kong

10 9 8 7 6 5 4 3 2 1

LIBRARY OF CONGRESS CATALOGING-IN-PUBLICATION DATA

DeSpain, Pleasant.
Strongheart Jack and the beanstalk / as told by Pleasant DeSpain;
illustrations by Joe Shlichta.
    p.   cm.
Summary: In this version of the classic tale, Jack climbs the magic beanstalk
with a wise cat who helps him kill the giant, rescue his true love, and regain
his father's fortune.
ISBN 0-87483-414-7: $15.95
[1. Fairy tales. 2. Folklore—England. 3. Giants—Folklore.]
I. Shlichta, Joe, ill.   II. Title.
PZ8.D473St   1995
398.2´0942´02—dc20
[E]   94-45815

The paper used in this publication meets the minimum requirements of the
American National Standards for Information Sciences—
permanence of Paper for Printed Library Materials, ANSI.48-1984

About the Story

The myth of Jack, the lad who defeats giants, began in the British Isles in the third century. From early historian Geoffrey of Monmouth, we learn that this nursery tale was inspired by a metrical tale of Brutus, the supposed founder of the British race and kingdom.

My retelling is based on the earliest known versions and includes the "heart" of the tale, often omitted, involving the cruel history of the giant and Jack's family prior to the time the story begins.

The character called Jack has since traveled wherever the British have settled. The Appalachian tale, "Jack and the Bean Trees," as recorded by Richard Chase, is a good example. Jack exists by other names in other cultures as well, but in this incarnation, he is particularly shaped by the British feudal system. One of the most popular classical fairy tales in the western world, this story demonstrates that the quest for justice, protection from brutal ruling forces, and happiness in life, continues. Action is required, and "everyman" Jack is the right person for the job.

This tale is written to be read aloud. The teacher or parent can narrate while the children enact the character roles. Create new riddles for the yellow tortoise to put to Jack. Have everyone repeat the giant's chilling phrases with gusto! Change and add to the plot. What would happen if the giant captured Jack? How would Elinor and Octavia rescue him?

And most importantly, ask why the main character is called Strongheart Jack. This may open important doors to the possibilities of human character.

—P.D.

Once upon a time, in the dark days of King Alfred's rule, there lived a lad named Jack. Everyone in the village called him Lazy Jack. Even his mother.

"Lazy Jack! Look at how poor we are! Winter is soon upon us and the roof needs thatching. We have little food, and except for one cow, we've sold our livestock. It breaks my old heart in two, but now we must sell Jewel as well. A milking cow with no milk left won't bring much, but do the best you can. Take her to the city and bring the money straight home to me."

"Oh, Ma," replied Jack, "I'm too tired. I'll sell her tomorrow."

"You'll go now, or I'll beat you with this broom!"

Jack set off for market with Jewel in tow. He stopped to rest at every turn in the road, and it wasn't long till twilight.

"Ho there, Jack!" came the scratchy voice of an old tinker. The tinker's wagon was full of pots and pans and other goods to sell along the way.

"Ho right back at you, Tinker Man. Have a rest and we'll talk about yesterday, today, and tomorrow."

"A fine tongue for words, haven't you, Jack? And what of that fine cow? Where are you taking her?"

"To market. I'm going to sell her for three gold coins!"

"Why go all the way to town? Sell her to me and I'll give you what's in this bag."

The old man took a small satchel from inside his tattered shirt and poured its contents into his hand. "Beans, lad. Seven sparkling and mysterious beans. Far more valuable than a mere three coins. Think of it, Jack. With these in your hand, who knows what magic you can do?"

"But my mother said . . ."

"Your mother will be proud of you, son. It's out of the ordinary that we get the extraordinary! Deal?"

"Done!" said Jack.

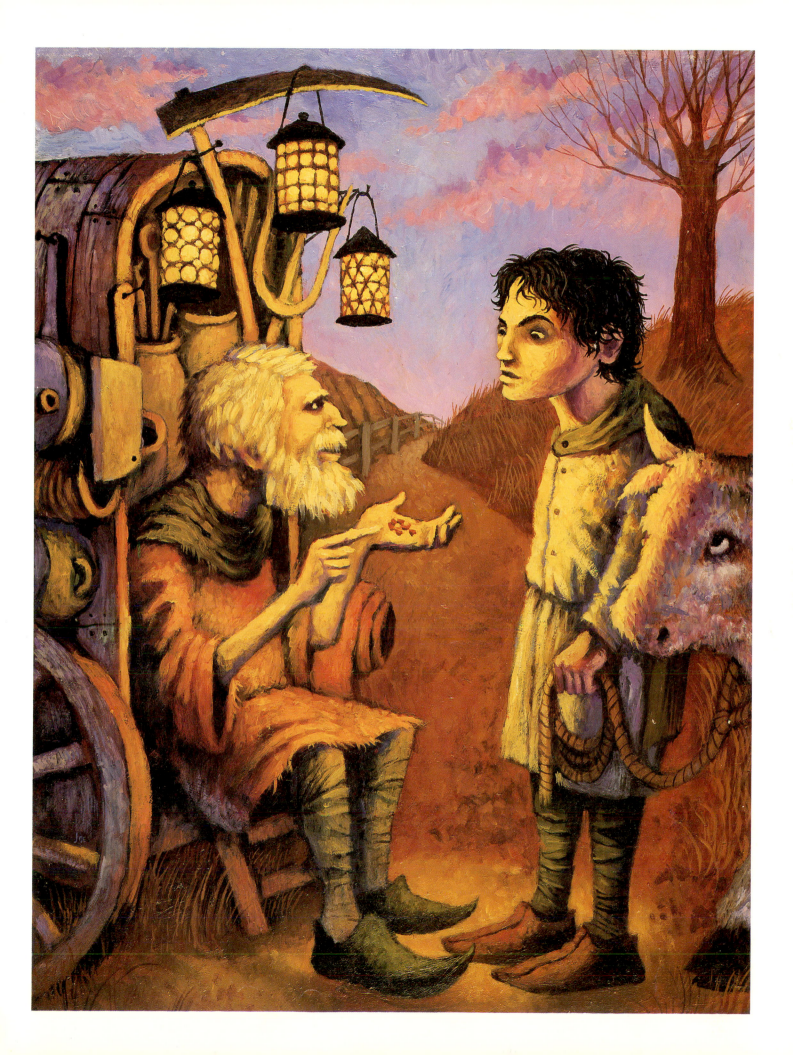

Twilight melted into night, and he ran back to the village.

When his mother saw the beans, she was enraged. "You lazy lout!" she cried. "How could you be so gullible? Seven beans for Jewel? Seven ordinary beans?"

"But Mother, they're magic! The tinker said . . ."

"I'll show you magic." She flung the beans out the open window into the garden. "Off to bed with you, Jack, and if you're hungry, feast on your bargain. I'm disappointed in you, and scared for us. Out of my sight!"

Jack climbed the ladder to the loft and lay on his pallet. He heard his mother weeping and calling out, "Oh, Jerold, what are we to do?"

Jerold was the name of his father, a man he had never known. Whenever Jack asked about him, his mother looked sad and shut her mouth tight. Her silence on the subject was as strong as a rock wall. At long last, Jack slipped off into the land of dreams.

The seven sparkling beans, however, were not at rest. A fat rain cloud floated above the garden and spilled its contents onto the fertile soil. The beans snapped open, one by one, and began to sprout. Down deep into the ground grew their anchoring roots. Up high into the sky climbed their flying shoots. Then each of the seven intertwined into a single, sturdy stalk. Broad leaves unfolded from the tendrils and formed a thin canopy. When the top of the beanstalk broke through the highest cloud, its magic was complete.

The next morning, the sparrows chirped excitedly as they fluttered around the new spire of green. Jack awakened and peeked outside. He rubbed his eyes and looked again. "Mother, Mother! Wake up! Look out the window! The beans *were* magic! See the stems . . . they form a ladder. I'll climb it, Mother. There is something up there for us. I know it."

Jack's mother tried to stop him, but after an hour of futile pleading she realized he wouldn't listen. She removed her husband's silver sword from the mantle, saying, "Carry it with you, Son. May it help bring you safely home."

The boy accepted the sword and ran his fingers over the ornate letters carved into the handle. *Sir Jerold*, it read. Jack felt a burst of energy rush through his fingers and travel directly to his pounding heart.

"Thank you, Mother."

With knapsack, water flask, and sword, the youth began his quest. Higher and higher he ventured, and soon he was out of sight.

Octavia, the village cat, leaped from the ground to the beanstalk and began to climb up after him. She was a calico cat— her belly and legs were painted bright white. Red then black swirled over her back and tail. The eighth born, Octavia knew many things, including the history of Jack's family. She leaped upwards from branch to branch.

Suddenly, danger struck. A flock of cawing crows flew out of a cloud and dove at the cat, trying to knock her from her perch. Octavia yowled!

Jack fumbled for his sword and swayed out into space. He held tight, regained his balance, and climbed down to her rescue. The crows scattered and flew away. "Silly cat! What are you doing up here in birdland? If you're coming along, you'd better ride in my knapsack."

Octavia purred, snuggled into the dark leather bag, and was carried the rest of the way.

"This is strange . . ." murmured Jack, leaping from the top of the vine onto the hot sand of a desert floor. A thousand and ten cactus plants stood tall and proud all round them. "Most strange, indeed . . ."

"Stop," said a cactus standing before him. "No one may proceed without the right word. Do you know the password, boy?"

"I'm not a boy, I'm a man," said Jack.

"Wrong word," said the lead cactus. "Let's stick him." Advancing, the cacti waved their spiked arms up and down.

"Help!" cried Jack.

"Wrong again!" replied the cactus, closing in.

Octavia struggled out of the knapsack. "The word is *water*, Jack," she said. "Say *water* and give them a drink from your flask."

"Water!" Jack yelled, and he let them drink from his flask.

"You and the cat and all of your friends may pass this way forever," said the largest and oldest cactus.

Octavia jumped down from the sack, and across the desert sand they walked, a youth and his cat. And as they walked, they talked. Octavia had a story to tell . . .

"It's about your father, Jack, and why your mother won't tell you about him.

"Long ago, your father was a squire, and a good man indeed. Everyone respected Squire Jerold. Just as he was handsome, he was kind. And just as he was wealthy, he was generous. He lived in a fine manor house and owned all the surrounding farms. He loved riding horses, and was always good to cats. My mother, Serina, was his favorite. While riding one day, Squire Jerold met a strong-willed farm girl and fell in love. They married and were soon expecting a child. That was you, Jack."

"My father, a squire? What happened?"

"A huge and horrible man arrived one sad day. No one knew from where he came, and no one cared. His misshaped body and ugly face scared everyone off. All but your father. He offered the monster a place to rest and food to eat. The giant ate his fill, then cried out for more.

'Bring me blood! Bring me bone!

Bring me human! Then I'll return home!'

"Squire Jerold refused. And this is the hard part to tell, Jack. The giant killed and ate your father. Then he burned down the manor house and kidnapped your mother. The giant stopped to rest on the way home and fell asleep beside the road. Your mother escaped, taking your father's sword with her. My mother, Serina, followed her for ten days and nights until she came to the village in which you were born. It was on that day that she made an unshakable decision. Never would she tell you what had happened. She feared you would seek revenge and she doesn't want to lose you."

"Where does this giant dwell?" asked Jack.

"In the middle of the forest that lies beyond the sand dunes."

"How do you know?"

"I'm the eighth born, Jack. I often know the where of things."

Gripping his father's sword tight, Jack followed Octavia to the edge of the forest. Feeling a mixture of courage and fear, he realized that he wasn't lazy after all. He simply hadn't had a purpose before now. And more than a purpose, he sensed from deep within this was something he *had* to do.

They came to a calm pool of clear water. An ancient yellow tortoise greeted the travelers.

"Answer my riddle, the two of you, and a gift I'll give. What is round and flat, tall and small? What is filled with laughter and tears, bravery and fears?"

"The world is round and flat, tall and small," said Octavia.

"My heart is full of laughter and tears, bravery and fears," answered Jack.

"The world is your heart; your heart, the world!" said the tortoise. "You have answered well. Here is your gift: Love is stronger than might, stronger than fear. Keep your heart as strong as your sword, and right will triumph."

Jack thanked the tortoise, and he and Octavia continued their trek. At long last, a castle came into view. Massive and ugly, it could belong to no one but the giant. Three fiendish dogs, each savage and cruel, lay asleep in the sun, guarding the oaken door. From somewhere within the castle, a sad song was being sung.

"We must find a way in," said Jack.

"Shhh," said Octavia. "Let's let the sleeping dogs lie. They frighten me."

Jack made a plan and persuaded Octavia to help. First they sneaked behind the dogs and climbed the nearest tree. Then they tossed pebbles on top of the dogs' heads, one at a time. The dogs awoke and angrily began to blame each other for the trickery. A vicious fight began! Jack and Octavia ran to the castle door, pushed it open, and slipped inside.

They ran down a long and shadowy corridor leading to the kitchen. The singer of sadness was startled by the boy and his cat. A captive of the giant, the fair Elinor was up to her elbows in milk and flour. Stunned by her beauty and grace, Jack could not speak.

"Whoever you might be, you must flee this evil place!" cried Elinor. "The giant returns at any moment, and he eats intruders for supper!"

"Come with us," sputtered Jack.

"I cannot. My young brother is locked in the dungeon. The giant will eat him, as he did my mother, if I fail to cook his supper. Run while you can!"

The warning came too late for reasons two: the giant's approaching footsteps shook the castle floor, and Jack had fallen in love with Elinor.

"Hide! Climb into the onion bin! Your cat, too!"

"Fee! Fie! Foe! Fum!

I smell the blood of a hu-man!"

The horribly huge beast-of-a-man stomped into the kitchen. He searched the room with dark and wicked eyes set into a head too large for his thick neck. His stupendous ears were twice the size of his lumpy nose, and broken yellow teeth showed plainly through his sneer.

Elinor trembled at the sight and sound of him, but it was his smell that frightened her the most. It was the odor of decay that a thousand and one baths couldn't wash away.

"Of course you smell blood, Master," she said with a shaky voice. "You smell my blood, just as you do every night."

Never would she grow accustomed to his grotesque features and booming voice. Never did she realize that she was chained more securely to the castle than her brother!

Long before, the giant had stolen a golden Fairy Harp from the elves. Forged in the time of mystery, the harp could pluck her own strings and sing with an eerie beauty that made even the giant weep. The Fairy Harp held another power: she could cast spells at the command of her evil master. And her master had commanded that if Elinor set one foot beyond the castle wall, she would breathe no more.

The giant slurped up the remains of his meal, then belched. "Bring my Black Hen."

Elinor fetched the prize fowl and set her before the giant. The Black Hen laid golden eggs, one each night. But just as she clucked once, Jack began to sneeze. Onion dust danced about his nose, so he put his finger on his upper lip and clenched his teeth.

The hen clucked again, and Jack said, "Aaahhh . . ."

The hen clucked a third time, and Jack exploded. "*Chooo!*"

"What's that? Who's in with the onions? Elinor?"

"Just a cat, Master." She reached into the bin and pulled Octavia out. "She wandered into the castle today, and I was so lonely. Please let me keep her."

"*Purr . . . rr,*" said Octavia.

"Very well," said the giant. "But just for now. I may want her for my first course tomorrow night."

"Yeowwww!" screeched the cat as she dove back into the onions.

The giant threw back his shaggy head and laughed. Then be brayed, "I'm off to bed. Another glorious day of disruption awaits the sun!"

Jack and Octavia stayed the night in the onions, while Elinor slept upon her kitchen pallet. By the time they awoke, the giant was gone. Jack realized that he must act with haste.

Elinor showed him seventeen locked doors. "One of these leads to my brother. He's kept in the dungeon, and only the giant knows the passageway. He uses a silver key to open the lock, the key that hangs from the chain around his neck."

"I'll search for the secret door," said Octavia. "And purrrhaps there is another way in and out. I'm off to sneak and find."

Jack tried to persuade Elinor to run from the castle and hide in the woods until her brother could be set free.

She refused. "I must prepare the giant's feast, and it takes all the day."

Octavia discovered the proper door, but found no other way in. She soon returned to the kitchen. "It's the key or nothing, Jack. I hope you make a good thief."

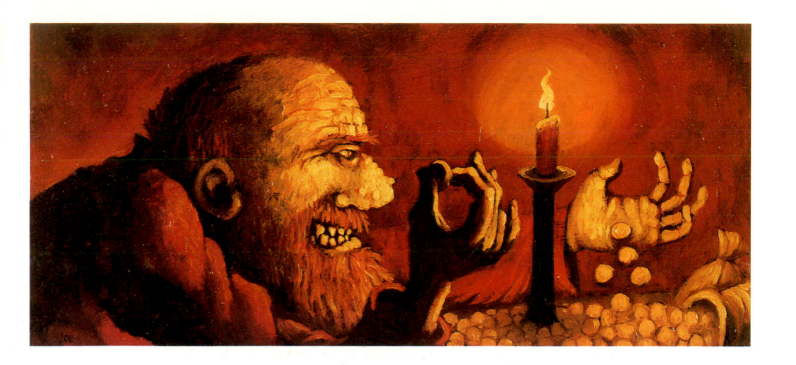

At twilight, the giant returned.

   "Fee! Fie! Foe! Fum!

   I smell the blood of a hu-man!"

"I know you do, Master," responded Elinor. "And I'm sure you can smell the pig I've roasted. Shall I fill your plate?"

Jack hid in a nearby closet and wore a necklace of garlic to keep the huge and sensitive nose at bay. He watched through a crack in the door. The monstrous man noisily ingested his food, then burped, and said, "Bring my bags of gold. I'll count myself to sleep."

After an hour of gloating upon his wealth, the giant fell into a deep sleep. Jack crept from the closet and climbed up onto the table. The silver key was in plain sight. Jack drew his sword and swung at the chain!

The giant awoke with a start. He grabbed at his neck and said, "Ouch! What's this? A mosquito with a hammer for a bite?"

Jack dove under the giant's elbow, barely escaping with his life. Soon the giant was snoring again. He awoke early in the morning and left for the day.

Jack was growing desperate. His love for Elinor was complete, yet they remained imprisoned. "My heart must be as strong as my sword," he murmured as he rigged a rope from a ceiling beam directly over the giant's chair.

Elinor boiled cabbage and wild hare, hoping to mask Jack's odor for one night more. She sang as she cooked, and all the forest knew of her love for Jack.

At end of day, the castle quaked.

> *"Fee! Fie! Foe! Fum!*
>
> *I smell the blood of a hu-man!"*

"Oh, Master," said Elinor, "you smell the cabbage. Sit and enjoy."

He slopped and gobbled till he could eat no more.

"Bring my fairy harp."

The harp played music strange and sweet, and even Jack, hanging from the rope above, shed a tear. The giant blubbered all the while, then closed his eyes, and began to snore. Hand over hand, Jack slipped down the rope until he reached the giant's thick neck. Carefully, he gripped, then lifted the chain that held the silver key, up and over the enormous head.

"Wake up! Master, wake up!" screamed the Fairy Harp. It was her duty to warn her keeper.

"Free your brother!" yelled Jack, as he tossed the key to Elinor. "The giant is mine!"

Lumbering from his chair, the giant laughed, "Yours, little man? I'll have you for a snack. And her brother will be my breakfast!"

Elinor ran to the dungeon door as Jack and the giant drew their swords. The giant was as slow as Jack was quick. The battle began with a crash! The giant cut the table in two, and Jack ran into the great hall. The beastly man followed and swung at Jack again and again, just missing the leaping youth. When the giant's blade stuck in the floor, Jack returned the attack, sharply slicing to and fro.

At last he hit home. The giant screamed and grabbed his bleeding big toe. He hopped all about, crying, *"Ouch! Ouch! Ouch!"* As he stumbled into a chair, he lost his balance and slowly toppled over. On the way down, he hit Jack broadside and sent him smashing through the castle door. Jack was knocked unconscious and lay still upon the ground.

Octavia leaped through the shattered door and hissed at the savage dogs, "Catch me if you can."

Ignoring Jack, the dogs chased after her, barking as they ran. The cat had earlier found a secret tunnel leading from the castle into the woods. She led the dogs inside, then doubled back and slammed the door. Octavia returned to the battle scene alone.

Opening the door to the dungeon, Elinor set her young brother free and gave him the Black Hen. "Run to the desert and beyond! Find the beanpole and climb down to earth. We'll catch up to you if we can!"

The boy fled past the giant and escaped into the night.

Elinor spied the giant's spilled blood, then saw her love fallen on the ground. "Jack!" she cried, and ran to him, unaware of the curse. Her first step outside, like her sharp intake of breath, was her last. Elinor fell dead at his side.

Jack stirred and sat up. As he gazed upon her he said, "You lie so still. Please, please awake."

Octavia grabbed at Jack's sleeve and pulled him away. "The battle's done. Come, Jack, run!"

Nearly blind with grief, Jack started down the path.

"You can't escape!" hollered the giant. "I'll catch you and your cat!"

From trail to tree, the chase was on. The giant limped slowly, but his steps were long. The distance between youth and beast was soon cut by half. They passed by the yellow tortoise and heard, "Onward, Strongheart Jack!"

Out of the woods and into the desert they ran, Octavia leading the way.

The giant roared, "You can't spill my blood, then run away. I recognize your silver sword, and I'll eat you whole like I did your father!"

Jack ran faster, yet closer the giant came. At last the edge of the sand appeared. The cacti saw them coming and made an opening for their friends. Jack grabbed Octavia, stuffed her into his knapsack, and leaped from the desert floor. He caught the top of the beanstalk with both hands and began a rapid descent. Fumbling and falling, he fought his way down. The earth was a distant goal.

The giant reached the cacti. *"Move!"* he demanded.

"Wrong word," said their leader. They began to stick his toes.

"*Ouch! Stop! Quit!*" pleaded the giant, and he stumbled over the edge into space. But as he fell, he grabbed at the beanstalk and was able to hold on tight. A smile crossed his cruel lips. The fight wasn't yet ended.

Jack was first to the ground. With sharp sword and strong heart, he chopped at the base of the stalk. Harder and faster he swung his blade, until the thick trunk was nearly cut through. The beanpole, so tall, leaned to the left then swayed far to the right. The monster held on tight. Then the stalk *cracked* in two!

"*NO!*" yelled the giant. Down and down he fell . . . When at last he hit the ground, the earth shuddered for a mile around. The dust slowly settled, and all was quiet. Jack peered over the edge of the new-made crater, and nodded his head. The giant was dead.

His mother and neighbors gathered round him. A small boy ran up to Jack and asked, "Where is Elinor? She's my sister."

Octavia struggled out of the sack and licked the tear from Jack's cheek. His love was forever gone, or so he believed. Suddenly, Jack heard a sweet sound from high, high, above.

"The Fairy Harp," he said.

Indeed it was. She sat on a castle shelf and rejoiced, for her master's evil commands no longer held their power. Now the dead could be brought back to life. She sang in reverse, and Elinor opened her eyes. She stood, stretched, and looked all about. "Where are you, Jack?" she asked.

Far below she saw him. The Fairy Harp called to Elinor, "Pick me up, and I'm yours to command."

Elinor did as she was asked, then said, "Take me to Jack." The golden strings plucked a rhythmic tune, its notes floating down to the earth. A strong tendril stirred from the broken stalk and began to soar toward the clouds. From its tip, a leaf, both broad and strong, unwound.

Harp in hand, Elinor stepped onto the leaf and was carried home. When she reached the ground, Jack embraced his own true love. "Marry me," he said.

"Yes, please," agreed Elinor.

Jack's mother beamed with pride.